Little MONSTER

This one's for Peter

Little M**O**NSTER

Allan Baillie

with illustrations by

David Cox

Text copyright © 1991 by Allan Baillie.
Illustrations copyright © 1991 by David Cox.
All rights reserved. Published by Scholastic Inc., 555 Broadway, New York, NY, 10012, by arrangement with Omnibus Books.
Printed in the United States of America CGB

ISBN 0-439-08087-8

8 9 10 11 12 13 14   23   12 11 10 09

Contents

1

Roger

For a start, it's Sonia's fault. So I don't feel sorry for her or guilty or anything, not at all.

If she hadn't made all that fuss about the bug in her hair—and it was only a small bug, too— Ms. Price wouldn't have marched me out to the school garden and made me weed her roses when everyone in the world was going home. And I wouldn't have found this furry caterpillar munching away at a leaf, and I wouldn't have been late.

Mom wouldn't have been worrying about where I was, and wouldn't have poured salt instead of sugar into the cake she was making. Then she wouldn't have sent me down to the store to buy eggs and milk to start all over again. And then I wouldn't be sitting on the curb near the store trying to remember what it was I was supposed to get, and watching my furry caterpillar crawl up my arm, when Roger showed up.

You see, it's *all* Sonia's fault.

Anyway, this caterpillar is tickling my arm like

a hundred ants, and I'm thinking of flicking it off and introducing it to Sonia, when this odd kid weaves down the pavement.

Now, I haven't seen the kid before. I figure he's just moved into the neighborhood, so I get ready to give him the nod. I do this all the time. I mean, you don't want to make enemies to start off with, do you? He might have brothers who bend bars with their teeth, or a father who's got a stable full of horses that need riding. . . .

But this kid, I mean he's *weird!*

I don't mean he's got green skin or wears a suit like Batman. No, nothing like that. Oh, he's a bit on the tall side. Maybe he gets away with combing his hair only once a month. Maybe those green eyes are just a little wide. And the shirt changes color as he moves. And he's wearing long socks. But apart from all that, he's just a normal kid.

Except he keeps on waving his finger around, glaring at it, and talking to himself. And he's a bit twitchy. He's looking around all the time like he's being chased by a mob of gangsters.

So I don't say "Hi" to him.

So he walks into me.

I get knocked sideways, and he tries to keep walking. He tries to put his great flat foot on my face.

"Ow!" I yell.

He stops, peers at me and raises his foot. "Uh, hello. Sorry."

"That's okay, but . . ." I look at my arm. "My caterpillar's gone!" I start hunting around. I see it in the air, just dangling—a flying caterpillar?—and reach for it.

And it disappears. Poof! Just like that.

"Queeg!" says the kid, very annoyed.

I look at him. "My name's Drew," I tell him through my teeth. I think I may have to serve him a knuckle sandwich.

But he flaps his hands like they are white flags. "Sorry, Drew. Didn't mean you. I'm Roger."

"All right."

"But your caterpillar's gone. Forever. Was it a pet? Maybe we can find another."

I get up. "Nah. Who'd want to keep a dumb caterpillar for a pet? You're new here, right? Where do you live?"

"I don't really live here. I'm only here for a day. We have to move on, always moving on."

"Oh. Too bad," I say.

"Yeah, a pity." He sounds sad. "It's Dad's business . . . Get away!"

I take a step back. "Alright, alright."

He blinks at me. "I don't mean you. Want some ice cream?"

Okay, most times I'm smart. Most times I would see that this kid Roger is setting up some sort of trap. If I'm smart, this is the time I shake my head, say "Thanks, but no," and walk away. But this time I forget to be smart. . . .

"Uh, yeah," I say.

So Roger drags me into the ice cream store.

Len stops polishing his candy jars and smiles at us.

"Three chocolate ice cream cones, one with sprinkles, please. Don't do that," he says to Len behind the counter.

Len stares at Roger and stops smiling.

But Roger turns to me. "Sorry, Drew, I should ask you what you want."

"That's all right. Chocolate is fine." "Three?" Len looks a bit confused. "Yes, three."

Len raises an eyebrow at me, sort of asking, "What's with this kid, anyway?" I wrinkle my nose, sort of saying: "I don't know *anything* about this one."

Anyway, Roger and I walk to the end of the road. We stop at a patch of rocks. I sit down and get on with the ice cream wrecking job. Roger goes to another rock and puts the ice cream cone with sprinkles in a pile of pebbles. Then he comes over and joins me.

"For the ants?" I say.

"Yeah, well—" Then he sweeps his ice cream high above his head. "No, no! Over there!"

A large bird lands near the ice cream in the pebbles, gives it a beady-eyed look, and shuffles sideways. Then it shrieks and flaps *backwards* into the air. It flies to an old tree and complains to everyone for a long time.

I'm trying to figure things out. "Uh, did you throw a stone at the bird?" I ask Roger.

"No."

I feel better because *I* didn't see anything. "What's your dad do?" I say politely.

He looks secretive. "Oh, he buys and sells, buys and sells. From anywhere."

"Anywhere? From all over the world?" I give him a tiny smirk.

"More," he says.

Then the cone with the sprinkles rises from the rock and hangs in the air. Like it's a balloon.

"Hey, that's a fantastic trick!" I'm just about falling off my rock.

"Yes, a trick . . ." Roger is carefully looking at his shoes. "Sometimes Dad makes bad deals. Sometimes."

Some of the floating ice cream has disappeared.

"How *do* you do that, Roger?" I'm shouting.

Roger raises his head and gives me a funny look. "Would you like to do a trick like that, Drew?"

"Oh yes! Hey, that's great. Show me!"

"I suppose Dad wouldn't mind getting rid of it. But it'll cost you."

"Oh." I remember I've got a pocket full of money. But it's Mom's money.

"That a problem, Drew?"

The bottom of the ice cream cone snaps off and vanishes.

"How much?" I ask miserably. I know I've got to have that trick. It's going to cost everything I've got. Mom will hit the roof when I go home without anything. And then Dad will yell at me until the middle of next week. . . .

"Got a nickel?" Roger says, like he has a mouth full of honey.

"Oh, yes!" I slap the coin into Roger's hand before he can change his mind.

"But it has to be a secret, forever."

"Yes, yes, come on!" I can't see any wires. The ice cream is being sucked into the bottomless cone.

"But I have to warn you. You might not like to keep it."

"I like it, I like it."

"And maybe you won't be able to give it away."

"I don't want to give it away! Come on, what

is it?"

Roger smiles happily and rubs his hands together. "Well, that's it, then. You just say after me: Queeg, I am."

"Huh? Quark, I—"

"No, no. Queeg. It has to be Queeg."

"Queek."

"Queeg."

"Queeg."

"Right, good. Queeg, I am . . ."

"Queeg, I am . . ."

". . . your new rightful owner."

". . . your new rightful owner."

"And that's it." Roger flips my coin into the air and leaps to his feet.

"That's it? *That* is the trick? That's nothing at all."

"Look at the ice cream."

"Look at the ice cream . . ." I stop and screech: "There's a red and purple *thing* eating it!"

"Yes. But I can't see it any more. It's yours." Roger walks quickly away. "Have fun," he calls back. Then he is gone.

2

Queeg

Okay, there you are sitting on a rock, staring at something impossible, with claws, fangs and wings. And it is slurping an ice cream cone. What do you do?

"Hello," I say.

"Gnfflm," it says. It grins. Like it is saying: "When I finish the ice cream, I am going to start eating you."

Except it isn't big enough. It's only the size of a basketball, a basketball with a head, claws, fangs and wings. Maybe it's trying to give me the evil eye with that big yellow stare. Mostly it looks like it's sitting on a thorn and is trying to remember how to get off. The claws? Well, they are good enough for the ice cream cone, but you wouldn't tackle an angry kitten with them. And the wings are too small to fan a beetle. Forget about flying.

"You are ridiculous," I say. "You don't exist."

"Gnffle," it says, and shoves the last of the ice cream cone into its mouth.

I look around for Roger, because he still has to

be close to make this thing work. But he isn't here. When I look back, the thing is still here. It is scratching its fat little belly and burping happily.

So I go over to the creature and help it scratch. It giggles at me, something like a bubbling stew.

"Cute little monster," I say.

"Pook gnffle."

Then I scratch it behind its bat ears.

And it bites me on the thumb.

I yell at it, pull my thumb away and hop around for a bit. When I look at the thumb, it's still there. It isn't bleeding, but it hurts.

"I ought to kick you," I say, and lift my foot.

It goes wide-eyed and rolls across the rock, sniffling.

"Don't get cute with me," I say. "You're just a little monster. I have better things to do than be bitten to death by you." And I turn around and walk from the pet nightmare Roger has tried to give away.

I hear shuffling behind me. I look and the little monster is walking after me. With big sad eyes.

"Don't you try that with me. You've taken your last nibble off me. Get lost." I wave at it, stamp at it.

It waves back and stamps its webbed foot in the dust.

"Go away!" I walk away very fast, my pocket clinking heavily.

It walks even faster, rocking like an egg that's about to fall.

About then I remember what Roger made me say. "I am *not* your rightful owner! Go back to Roger!"

That doesn't do any good. I start to run, sounding like an army of charging tin men.

There's also the sound of a dozen mosquitoes behind me. I look back and it's gone. That's that.

Except the dozen mosquitoes are above my head and that little monster is flying. You can't see those tiny wings any more, just a blur.

"Oh," I say, and slow down.

The little monster flies to my side. The wings flutter on its back. It is panting.

"I just can't get rid of you, eh?"

It reaches up for my hand, catches my fingers with its claws, opens its mouth with the gleaming fangs.

"Ow! Stop!"

It pushes out its long purple tongue and licks my thumb.

"You saying sorry?"

And it blinks those big eyes at me.

Well, maybe it's not such a bad thing to have a monster around the house. Could be sort of fun.

It gives me a final lick, like being rubbed with wet sandpaper.

"What was your name? Queeg? Come on, let's go home."

3

Home

I was sort of looking forward to walking into the house with Queeg behind me. Mom would maybe scream and drop things, but it would be worth it.

Mom is sitting at the computer in her room as I come in the back door.

"Hi Mom," I yell.

She bustles into the kitchen and stirs a bubbling pot. "Where have you been, Drew? Wipe your feet. Where are my eggs and milk?"

"Oh. I forgot."

"You forgot? Why do you think you were sent down to the store? For heaven's sake, talk about forgetful . . . Never mind, I'll bake the cake tomorrow."

"But this is better. Look what I brought home."

Mom squints and waves her spoon at me. "And *what* have you brought home? You know you aren't allowed to bring anything home. Not after that wild muddy sheep-dog. Your father will—"

"This." I step to one side and Queeg is snorting

14

in the doorway.

Mom brushes past me, almost steps on Queeg, and peers out the door. "Where?"

"Mom! You're almost standing on it!"

Mom takes a quick step backwards and looks down at Queeg. She frowns and looks sideways at me. "There's nothing there."

"There is too!"

"Uh, what is supposed to be here, Drew?"

"My monster! It flies and—watch out—it bites."

Mom nods wisely. "Oh, yes, I see it now." She looks straight over Queeg's head. "Horrible monster, so big . . ."

"Big?"

"Bigger than the house, and those teeth! We'd better feed it before it eats us."

Sometimes parents are so embarrassing, aren't they?

I sigh. "It's all right, Mom. He's not hungry now."

I go into my room. Queeg lies on my bed and catches flies with his tongue.

This is great, I think. Nobody can see Queeg but me. I've got the world's only invisible monster. This is getting better and better!

I fiddle with some homework—math and spelling. "You wouldn't be a magic monster, would you Queeg?"

"Burrple," says Queeg.

"You know, like a genie in a bottle? Okay, you don't have a bottle, but you're just as fantastic as a genie. If you're a magic monster, then you have to give me three wishes, and they'll come true. Right?"

"Gennerff," says Queeg.

I know the rules. "Okay, Queeg, I wish to be able to fly. And none of this funny stuff. I don't want feathers, or a propeller on my nose. I want to fly like Superman. Right?"

"Ffnlfe," says Queeg.

"Ffnlfe? That sounds like something. A little magic, hey?" I step away from the desk and climb up on the bed. I stand on the edge and wave my arms about. "Now, just a little flight, to get the feel of it. Up—up—and—awayyy!"

I crash down to the floor.

"What's going on up there?" Mom yells.

"Nothing, nothing!" I slide back into my desk.

Queeg tilts his head and sort of frowns.

"Okay, you're not a magic monster," I say. I should have figured *that* out. If Queeg was in the business of granting wishes, Roger would never have let him go. Anyway, why *did* he let Queeg go?

I give Queeg the hard stare. "Well, what can you do?"

About that time Sir Harry, Mom's cat, slides in with a sneer. Sir Harry and I don't get along because he thinks that cats are smarter than people and that he is a Superior Being and I am dumber than a mouse. According to Sir Harry, I was invented to feed and entertain him, and I'm failing at both jobs. He reminds me of Sonia.

I wad up a piece of paper into a ball and throw it at Sir Harry's head. Sir Harry ducks and arches his back. Queeg catches the paper ball in the air, zooming around like a very fat mosquito.

Sir Harry stares at the ball in Queeg's claws

and stands up on his rear legs and tries to hit it. Queeg plays with the ball just beyond Sir Harry's paws until Sir Harry overreaches and tumbles on his back. Queeg flops back on the bed and giggles. Sir Harry glares at *me*.

"You're a joker, Queeg," I say, and grin at him. Maybe I can train my monster like a puppy.

Then Mom breezes in and just about steps on Sir Harry's tail. "Who are you talking to, Drew?"

I think very fast for a moment. Sometimes the brain comes up with great ideas from absolutely nowhere. "Oh, just Queeg," I say.

"Queeg? Oh, your monster."

"Yes, Queeg."

Mom looks over my shoulder. "Well, Queeg can't be helping you with your homework. What's $34x + e9$?"

"What's what?"

"That's what you've got in your book."

"Oh, yes. Um."

"You just forget about Queeg until you've done your homework. Correctly." And she sails out again.

See what I mean about the brain? I got out of that one really fast. No, I don't mean about the homework. I mean about Mom. She thinks I'm playing with an imaginary monster. She won't worry when I talk to it.

It even works when Dad comes home.

After I finish my homework I get to watch TV—with Queeg. Queeg likes cartoons but he cheers for the wrong side. When the cat is creeping up on the canary with a vacuum cleaner, Queeg laughs away happily. When the little old lady snatches the canary from the cat's mouth and belts the cat with a broom, he makes a sound like a small foghorn.

Anyway, when I change the channel, he gets very interested. He waddles over to the TV and changes it back.

"Not that one, Queeg!" I shout and almost spill my milk.

Dad walks through the front door with a long box. "I'm home!"

Queeg looks at the screen and reaches for the knob.

Dad shoves his head and his box into the den. "Rrroom! Vrey!"

These days Dad makes model planes at home. We try to ignore him.

Queeg changes the channel again.

"That's better. Hi, Dad."

"Wait till you see what I've got . . ." Dad frowns. "How'd you do that?"

Mom calls from the kitchen: "Don't mind Drew,

he's playing monsters."

"Oh." Dad steps sideways toward the kitchen, looking a little lost. "I didn't know we had a remote control. . . ."

Queeg grabs my glass of milk and starts to drink it. I grab it back very quickly and grin at Dad as he backs, blinking, into the kitchen.

It's beautiful. I can't wait until I take Queeg to school.

4

School

The next day on the way to school, I am teaching Queeg how to play soccer with a pebble, when Joe strolls up. You wouldn't say he was skinny, but he can hide behind a TV antenna. He's so tall he's got to duck for incoming planes. Anyway he's my friend, most of the time. Even when I have to look after him, which is most of the time.

I kick the pebble out of the way and say, "Alright, Queeg, stop now."

"Who are you talking to?" Joe runs up to the pebble, black hair flopping all over the place, and just about tramples Queeg. He kicks the pebble out of sight.

Queeg gives a sad little sigh and comes to my side.

"My monster," I tell Joe. Why not let everyone into my little game? Makes it all so easy.

Joe snorts and holds his hand to his face and tiptoes past Mrs. Brown's gate. "What monster?" he says when we're safely past. "You mean you can talk to Mrs. Brown's mutt?"

"Nah, I got a monster of my own." I point at Queeg. "There. Queeg." Yes, yes, I know that Joe can't see him. But that doesn't matter, does it?

"Uh, stop carrying on like a little kid. I'm getting a new bike!"

Maybe I should think about this. Okay, Mom thinks I'm being a cute kid with my monster game. Dad doesn't much care so long as I don't fiddle with his glue. But the kids aren't going to think I'm cute. They are going to think I've fallen on my head from a tall tree.

Queeg has to stay a secret. I can't have a monster making a dummy out of me.

"Just fooling around, Joe. Hey, when do we see the bike?"

"It's a birthday present. Day after tomorrow. Vram— varoom! Come on, we'll be late for school."

We get to school as the bell rings, and run to the back of the assembly. Queeg flaps around us and lands on Joe's head by mistake. Joe frowns and sweeps his arm over his head, knocking Queeg to the ground. Joe looks up at the sky as he runs his fingers through his hair. Queeg picks himself up and prepares to bite Joe on the ankle.

"No!" I hiss at Queeg and point a finger at him.

But Sonia Theraby—yes, she's the one I was

talking about in the beginning—is staring at me with the makings of a sneer stuck on her face. Now, Sonia thinks she looks like a movie star—a different one every week—and carries on as if she were one. I think she looks like a horror movie star (a different one every day) and we don't get along.

Anyway, to throw Sonia off, I point at the sky where Joe was looking. But Joe is now looking at his fingers. I just wiggle my fingers at her for something to do.

Sonia hits me with the full sneer. "You're late."

"Wasn't."

"Was."

"Wasn't."

"Quiet, children . . ." mutters Ms. Price from the side.

The principal starts talking. Another day has started. Queeg listens for a while and then begins to copy the principal. Not the words, you understand, but just the sound and the rhythm of the principal's voice, using little monster sounds.

Something like: "Wurfle wurfle wingy purpif brim."

After you hear that for a while it's very hard to avoid laughing. The only way to avoid being caught laughing is to cough. So I cough and Sonia wrinkles her nose. Ms. Price glares, and Joe wonders what is going on.

And Shay, a kid built like a brick garage (and about as bright), starts to frown at me and shows his fist.

This is serious. I try to smile at him, which only makes things worse. I mean, have you ever tried to smile at the same time as you are coughing to hide the giggles? I am getting purple around the ears.

We finally start to march into school. Shay bumps me. "What's so funny about me, Squirt?"

"Nothing, Shay, really nothing."

Queeg bites Shay on the ankle. I have to go into another burst of coughing. So Shay pushes me into

Sonia. Sonia squeals like she is being murdered. Ms. Price wiggles a finger at me as we go into the class.

When we sit down, Ms. Price looks at me as if *I've* turned into a monster.

"Finished coughing, Drew?" she says.

"Yes, Ms. Price. Sorry, Ms. Price." Queeg is happily chewing on my shoelaces.

"He wasn't coughing," said Sonia. "He was laughing."

"That's enough, Sonia. What was so funny, Drew?"

"Oh, nothing, nothing at all."

"All right. Open your books."

Well, it's not a good start to the day, but things have to get better. Don't they?

5

Little Monster Acts

I try to forget about Queeg and concentrate on Ms. Price, but she isn't helping. She talks about states and cities and how big they are. That's enough to put a kid to sleep.

Someone snores.

Ms. Price turns to me. Any more of this, Drew, and you are in big trouble."

"I didn't . . . I wasn't . . ." Was I?

Ms. Price turns to the blackboard. Shay is staring at me. Sonia is in a mess of confusion. She is lifting her nose to show her disgust for Shay's snore. At the same time she is trying to curl her lip at me.

Queeg lets go of the shoelaces and waddles over to Ms. Price's table, watching as she draws a map of Australia. I realize I don't know much about my monster. I could be in trouble here. Queeg could be getting ready to bite Ms. Price on the leg, land on her head, lick her on the finger . . . I am not feeling very well.

When she's not looking, Queeg picks up a piece

of chalk and puts Sydney in the sea. Nobody notices what has happened until Sonia points it out. She would.

Ms. Price frowns, corrects the map, and Queeg wanders back to my feet and goes to sleep. I am feeling very weak.

At recess, Joe and I are sitting on a seat discussing the power ratio of ten gears on a bike, over a couple of candy bars. Queeg is sitting quietly on my foot.

Then Shay wanders over. "What are you doing?" he says.

"We're not snoring," I say.

"What do you want?" Joe says.

Shay looks hurt for about a second. Then he snatches a candy bar from my lunch box. "Pay day!" he yells.

"Put that back!" Joe leaps to his feet.

"Make me!" Shay pushes him back to the seat.

I grab Joe and hold him on the seat until Shay races off with my candy bar to play baseball.

I never try to get things back from Shay. That's about as smart as playing "chicken" with a bus. Like I said, Joe is my friend, but he keeps thinking he's a superhero and I have to keep on saving him.

We have the usual argument. Joe peels off to get Shay in the baseball game. About then I realize that Queeg has moved from my shoe and is following Shay.

Oh, it's great. Shay is at bat, and Joe is pitching. Shay prepares to hit the ball out of the schoolyard. He pounds the ground with his bat like it's a club. Joe is looking nervous as he winds up for the pitch.

The ball flies toward the catcher, and Shay is growling.

Queeg is buzzing around like a fat bee. He catches the ball before it reaches Shay's bat. Shay swings, misses, and hits the air instead. Queeg waves the ball in front of Shay's nose.

I'm rolling around on my seat, trying to get a breath between giggles, when Sonia pushes me off.

"Silly boy," she says, and walks into class like a princess.

Later, she is painting a picture of a house on a piece of paper. Queeg stands on the paper. He gets his feet painted instead of the paper, but Sonia can't see this. She sees me watching, sniffs at me, and while she is sniffing, Queeg walks away.

She spends a long time trying to figure out how the white webbed footprints got on her lovely painting.

I walk home after school with Queeg worfling beside me. I think that this has definitely been about the best day in my life. Train Queeg? He doesn't need training, or anything at all.

"You're all right, Queeg," I say. "Don't know what's supposed to be wrong with you. You're a great monster."

Well, that was what I said. Then.

6
Dad's Model

Things start going a little wrong that night. And it's all Dad's fault.

Dad comes home early with a little box. He's whistling. He can't whistle. He sounds like a dented steam kettle, but that's what he's trying to do.

"Hello, Gorgeous One!" he says to Mom. He picks her up, squeezes her like some great grizzly bear and nibbles her ear.

"Hello, son!" Dad beams at me.

I walk backwards in a hurry.

"What have you been doing at school today? Never mind, come on, I'll show you what *I've* been doing while you've been snoring in bed."

Now, having Dad around is like having a mad scientist in the house. Very interesting, but just a little scary. When he goes off to work he wears a dull gray suit and does something very boring with numbers. When he comes back, he changes into ragged shorts and goes off into his special room. Nobody, but *nobody* gets into that room without the royal nod. That is about as rare as Ms. Price giggling.

I trot after Dad. He is so excited about the little box that he is still wearing the gray suit. And for the moment I forget about Queeg.

Dad swings the door open and turns on the light. The place stinks of glue and paint and oil. There are a few old plastic models of boats held together by spiderwebs. There are wooden models of sailing ships which have a few spiderwebs. Then there are planes which don't fly, but dangle from the ceiling and pick up dust. There are gliders that cling to the wall. I have seen all these before.

There is the skeleton of a plane on the table. It is as big across as I can reach. It is made of thin pieces of wood and wire covered in plastic. There is a small black box with wheels and a battery in the skeleton.

"What do you think?" Dad says.

"Uh, it's nice." I'm being polite. I'm about to be even more polite, but Queeg flutters up to my shoulder. "Yerk!" I say.

"You don't understand," Dad says. "This one flies!"

Queeg flaps his wings about my right ear.

"Stop that!" I say.

Dad gives me a funny look. "You think I'm

joking?" He grabs a thing with buttons all over it and an antenna. He pushes some of the buttons. The wires move around the wheels and things on the wings, and the tail wobbles. "See?"

"That won't fly. It's got too many holes," I say. I know all about these things. I have folded great paper gliders.

"Uh, but it gets its skin tonight. And this!" Dad opens the little box and pulls out a funny piece of metal.

Queeg says, "Murfel quel?" in my ear so I bump him with my head. He wobbles off my shoulder.

"A little parachute?" I try.

Queeg flaps around Dad's head.

Dad frowns a bit. "No, no. It's an engine."

Queeg flies up to a plastic plane dangling from the light and sits on it. The shadow of the plastic plane moves around.

Dad shoves a large propeller on one end of the engine. "Don't do that, Drew."

"I'm not." If anything happens and they don't know what's causing it, they always blame you for it. Did you ever notice that?

"Well, don't." Dad puts his little engine into the vice he has on the table, and pours gasoline or something into it from a small, flat tin.

I get interested. Queeg gets interested and flies

down from the plane. Dad flips the propeller.

"Watch it . . ." He keeps flipping the propeller. The engine begins to cough.

"Contact," he says. No, I don't know what he means, but the propeller suddenly spins so fast it disappears. The engine purrs like a box full of Sir Harrys. "There we are."

Except there is no propeller anymore, just a very strong breeze. So Queeg investigates, puts his nose closer—

"No, Queeg!" I yell, and reach for the little monster.

Queeg yelps and bounces to the floor, hits the plastic plane, bounces off that, becomes caught on one of the tall wooden ships, and blows his nose.

"What happened?" Dad yells at me. He yells too soon. Things are still happening.

The propeller spins off the engine and hits Queeg on the tail. Queeg yelps again and jumps to the floor. The plastic plane spins around and drops, but Dad takes a long step and catches it. The long step thumps down on Queeg's webbed foot. Queeg is about to yelp again, but the ship he was caught in falls on him with a huge crash.

Dad turns the engine off and the room is silent.

I stoop and pick the shipwreck off Queeg.

"Yes . . ." Dad looks around him as if he doesn't

recognize the room at all. "I don't know," he says. "I just don't know."

Queeg climbs to his feet and fixes those lemon eyes on me.

"It's alright," I say.

"Alright? Alright!" Dad is almost screaming at me. He shakes his head, talks to himself. "No, no, you can't do that. Calm down. Go away, watch the news, see what disasters have happened to other people. Come back later. Yes."

Dad pushes me out of his special room and Queeg wurfles beside me.

But when I was looking into Queeg's lemon eyes, they seemed to be a bit angry.

7

A *Little* Revenge

Dad turns the TV on and collapses in his armchair.

Queeg sits back on his tail on the carpet and examines his nose.

And gets knocked sideways by Mom opening the door. It's not a good day for monsters.

"What fell?" says Mom.

"Nothing, nothing. I'll fix it later."

Mom opens her hands and looks at the ceiling. She goes out the door and knocks Queeg onto his tail again. The news starts. Queeg picks himself up and marches to the TV and changes the channel to a game show.

"Drew . . ." Dad warns.

"Wasn't me," I say and quickly change it back. I walk to my chair smiling peacefully at Dad. I hear the click of the TV behind me.

"Drew!"

Click, click, clickety-click. Queeg is playing the TV like a video game.

"It's not me! It's *him*!" I kick Queeg away from

the knob. Queeg bounces to the door, scowling at me upside down.

"Stop your silly monster games! Leave me and my news in peace! Go, go!"

I go. I know what's best for me. Then I notice that Queeg is not with me.

Mom shrieks from her little office. "Drew! Drew, what have you done?"

I scoot into Mom's office. She is writing some dull story about statistics. Rather, she *was*. On the screen of her computer her story has been replaced by a cartoon of many little monsters chasing a canary. The little monsters look

suspiciously like Queeg.

"What did you do to my computer, Drew?"

I swing at Queeg, sitting smugly on the table. He topples to the floor. "I didn't do anything—"

"This is not funny! Stop your silly game. Get my story back, now! People are waiting for it."

"I don't know . . ."

"You'd better know, Drew . . ."

As I reach out for the keyboard, the little monsters catch the canary and disappear. They are replaced by graphs and a dull story about statistics.

Immediately Mom pushes the "Save" button and steps back, trembling. "Don't you ever think of doing that again."

"Yes, Mom."

"All right, we'll have dinner now."

Except we are supposed to have roast chicken. When we go into the kitchen the oven door is open. The chicken is gone.

How do you explain that?

8

The Training of Queeg

After Dad's long hunt around the place for a hungry burglar or a very, very smart dog, we have baked beans for dinner. About then I decide that I can't live with a monster unless he is trained. So I simply have to train Queeg.

I leave home early next morning with a couple of bananas and Queeg. I even buy an ice cream cone covered with sprinkles from Len's shop. Len looks at me strangely as I leave.

We walk around for a little while. Then Queeg dives for the ice cream.

"No!" I yell. Well, it's almost a yell. Anyway, I keep the ice cream out of that thing's claws.

"Guffle?" Queeg says, disappointed.

"All right, no more free rides. Now you've got to work. Stay!" I walk off.

Queeg bounces after me with his big, lemon-eyes on the ice cream.

"No!" I stop and shake a finger at him. Queeg grabs my finger and licks it. "No, no. Stay! Stay or I'll eat *you*!" I back away, pointing the finger at him.

"Trrufley?" Queeg tilts his head and looks so sad that I think he might cry, but he stays where he is.

"Good boy. No, don't move yet. Stay . . ." And then I see what I'm doing.

I'm training Queeg to follow my command, as if he were a dog, right? And it's beginning to work. But I'm forgetting that the only person in the world who can see Queeg is me. So everyone: Dad, Ms. Price, Shay, even ghastly Sonia—*everyone*— is going to see odd little Drew shouting Stay! Come! Go! Attack! (especially for Shay) to nothing but empty air. They are going to think I've flipped my lid, I've watched too many cartoons, I'm going to race around and bite people.

Okay, I think a bit and the ice cream starts to drip over my hand. Queeg begins to shuffle forward. I raise the finger, and he stops.

"Uh," I say.

I think a bit more, and the ice cream drips a bit more, and Queeg starts rocking in misery.

"Come here," I say, and beckon.

Queeg tilts his head, says "Quirreffy?" and begins to gallop toward the ice cream, big lemon-eyes glowing.

The finger goes up.

Queeg stops with a skid and a mutter.

40

The finger beckons.

Queeg shuffles forward, watching me suspiciously now.

Finger up, Queeg stops; finger beckons, and Queeg is charging, panting.

Finger up—but this time it's too late. Queeg is all over my hand with that lightning purple tongue. The ice cream is in his little claws, and he's shuffling away fast.

"Uh, good monster, good, good," I say, making it sound as if I wanted him to do just that. Well, he *would've* gotten the ice cream in the end.

Now I've got the hang of training. First, get Queeg to do what you want by yelling at him while you make a sign. Then stop yelling at him and just make the sign. Then all you have to do is make up new signs.

When Queeg has finished his ice cream he gets excited about my signs, maybe even more excited than he was about the bananas. He probably thinks we are playing some funny Drew game, with me making the rules up as we go along.

Anyway, by the end of the second banana we've worked out a very slick communication system. One finger straight up means "stay where you are." A beckoning finger means "come here." A pointing finger means "go there." A finger on the nose means "be quiet." A hand held out means "give what you have to me." A hand held up means "stop whatever you are doing immediately." A closed fist means "attack!"

I want to invent more signs, but the bananas are gone, and we are running late for school. But there are enough. I'm looking forward to meeting someone, with my highly trained little monster bouncing around me.

The first person we meet is Shay.

9

Shay Gets His

Well, we sort of didn't meet Shay. He met us.

I am walking along the sidewalk, thinking of more signs. Queeg is humming and whistling at the same time. No, I don't know how he does that, but after all he *is* a monster. Anyway, he is full of cheer. I see Joe, far ahead, and yell for him.

Then there's this rumbling behind me, and a screech. "Scram, Squirt!"

I start to turn around.

Forget it. I get thrown out of my sneakers, and I'm looking at an upside-down tree for half a moment, then I'm all over the pavement. Books, lunch, and my bag all slide into the gutter. Queeg comes spinning out of the air and crashes into my ribs.

Shooting away from us is Shay, hunched on a skateboard like a runaway missile. He looks back at us and grins and shouts: "Stee-rike!"

I whip my hand up in the air and point at Shay's back. "Get him, Queeg!" I snarl, shaking a fist. "Get him good!"

But Queeg has already gone. He is running after Shay, growling, his feet scratching furiously on the pavement.

Joe looks at me lying there like a train crash, then at Shay scooting down toward him. He raises his fists.

Shay laughs and veers around him.

Queeg takes off, looking like a purple melon falling *up*. He flies past Joe. Joe ducks at the sound of the wings, frowning, looking around him. Joe wobbles for a bit, as if he is trying to decide whether to chase after Shay or to come over and help me. He decides to help me.

While he is running over, I am watching Queeg, now a little purple cloud over Shay's head. Shay runs around a corner and disappears.

"Are you all right, Drew?" Joe is standing over me, pulling on my arm.

"Yes, fine. Let go." I get to my feet and start to pick up things.

"Shay's a creep. I hope he falls off." Joe picks up my bag.

"He'll get his," I say.

At that moment, Shay zooms back into our street. Backwards. With his mouth open and his arms flapping around him like he is trying to fly.

"Showing off," says Joe and turns away.

Of course I am seeing the purple melon of Queeg on the skateboard with Shay. I say nothing.

The board turns and comes toward us. Shay is facing the same way as the board is moving now. He thinks he's in control again and begins to smile.

"Get out of the way!" Joe yells. "Here he comes again!"

But Shay doesn't stay on the sidewalk, oh no. The board swings sideways and climbs Mrs. Brown's wooden front fence.

"Ayee!" says Shay.

And the wire grid of Mrs. Brown's front gate.

"Ha-hay-hee-hee!" says Shay.

The gate swings open and Mrs. Brown's huge killer guard dog leaps across the front lawn.

"Aargh!" says Shay and shuts his eyes.

In fright, Queeg scoots the board around the dog, back out through the open gate and up the nearest tree. Queeg, the board, and Shay disappear with a crash into the leaves. Mrs. Brown's dog runs around the tree snarling, its jaws dripping.

"I didn't know you could do that," Joe says.

Queeg sticks his head out of the leaves, and for the first time ever he looks a bit worried. I beckon with my finger. Queeg looks at me, sort of frowns, and looks down at Mrs. Brown's dog. He remembers what the beckoning means and remembers that he can fly. He flaps to my shoulder.

"Worriful," he says.

"You *did* say Shay would get his, didn't you?" says Joe.

"Help . . ." says Shay, trembling somewhere in the leaves.

Joe looks at me. I look at Joe.

"When do I get to see your bike, Joe?" I say.

"Uh, tomorrow—Saturday. I'll ride around to your place . . ."

"When it quiets down."

"Yeah. When the noise stops."

Joe and I walk across the road, away from that noisy dog, which for some reason keeps on trying to climb a tree. Anyway, we are in a hurry for school.

10

Sonia's Nibble

School starts very quietly. I'm there on time, I don't talk to anybody. My homework has all been done. All this seems to have had a bad effect on Sonia Theraby, because she keeps giving me the evil eye. As if I'm doing these things to upset her. I would, but I'm not. Not this time. Anyway, she gets so involved in giving me the evil eye that Ms. Price has to tell her to stop.

"Sonia, get your eyes off Drew and back to the map," Ms. Price says.

Which starts everyone laughing. Sonia turns bright red.

A good start to the day.

It gets better when Shay walks in, all embarrassed, with leaves sticking out of him. Sonia gives me a smug glance, saying she knows that I was part of this and that Shay will get even.

But Shay won't even look at me. He tells Ms. Price that he's sorry he's late but he fell into a bush. Sonia looks as disappointed as Sir Harry when a bug gets away.

Meanwhile Queeg has gone to sleep on my shoe. For a while the world is quiet and perfect.

Then there's lunchtime. Oh, it starts all right. No, it starts perfectly. Joe and I are playing handball. Queeg is lying in the sun and watching us with his eyes half shut. Shay comes around the corner.

We stop. I catch the ball and get ready for a run around the schoolyard. But Joe grins up at Shay, as if Shay is his best friend, and gives a soft, puppy dog growl.

Shay blinks at Joe, then turns and slinks away.

We haven't told anyone about Shay being chased up a tree by a dog. Joe just told Shay that we may never tell—so long as he doesn't bother us. For now, we are the most powerful kids you could ever meet. Generals, emperors, even.

So Sonia had to show up.

She comes wandering from the candy store, licking an ice cream cone, and just stops and sneers. You can even *hear* the Theraby sneer. But we don't look.

"What do you think you're doing?" she says.

"Go away," I say.

"You know you're doing it all wrong."

"Who says?"

"I know. You're supposed to bounce the ball."

"We do it our way. Come on, Joe." I hit the ball at the wall and have to blow on my hand and dance around a bit.

The ball blasts off the wall. Joe just looks at it like it has nothing at all to do with him. Sonia squeals and tries to jump out of the way and gets herself hit by the ball. She shouts at me, and the ice cream falls from the cone.

Queeg has been sadly watching Sonia licking the stuff, but now zooms in to catch the falling ice cream.

"Gerroffle!" he says, and beams and opens his mouth.

Sonia, of course, doesn't see him. She sees only the ice cream somehow floating near her knee, and scoops it out of Queeg's claws with the cone.

"Ah hah!" she crows, as if she's just saved the world.

Queeg is making a grumbling sound.

"And as for you, Drew Peters! Look what you've done to my dress! Throwing your dirty ball at me just because I know more about your silly game than you do. That hurt, and it wasn't funny and I'm going to tell Ms. Price. . . ."

With that she sails off.

I shake my finger at her back. "See if I care!" I hunt for something stronger to say, but I can't think of anything. I'm so mad I'm shaking a fist in the air.

Queeg is off with a mutter and a growl.

I look at my fist and realize what I've done. "No, Queeg, no!" I run after the little monster before he can get me into terrible trouble.

Queeg reaches Sonia and opens his mouth with its rows of tiny gleaming teeth. I throw myself into the air, clutching at him. He clicks his teeth. I grab him. Sonia says "Ouch!" I sprawl on the ground behind her. She turns around and looks down at me.

"You bit me . . ." she says, rubbing the back of her leg.

"Oh, no. No." I shake my head and try to smile up at her, showing her that I am friendly. Really.

But the smile is not a good idea. She sees my teeth. "You did! You did! You bit me!" She runs away across the schoolground. "Help! Help! Crazy boy! Crazy boy! Get the nets!" So everyone in the school is looking at me as if I've escaped from the zoo. Everyone except Joe, who is bouncing the ball against the wall like he's been doing it by himself for years, like he never knew a crazy kid called Drew Peters, and he wouldn't want to know him now.

11

Ms. Price's Disaster

The bell finally rings. We all file into the classroom. I want to be a million miles away. Like in Alaska. Sonia shows Ms. Price a tiny red mark on her leg. Ms. Price looks at me and frowns and shakes her head. She doesn't say anything because it is a tiny mark. But Sonia is frowning. Every other kid in the world is staring at me. Except Joe. Shay even rolls his lips back to flash his teeth, and he thinks that's funny. Joe? He just scribbles in his workbook and ignores everything.

Meanwhile Queeg is sitting on the windowsill as if he has gone to sleep. I am watching him and thinking a lot. I am in trouble because of Queeg. Oh, sure, I made a few signs, but that didn't matter. That little monster went after Sonia because she took her ice cream back from him. Any minute now Queeg could take off again and get me in even more trouble.

I am watching Queeg on the window ledge. He is doing nothing at all. But I am watching him so hard that I get into trouble anyway.

"Well, Drew, what is it?"

I blink. "Yes, Ms. Price?"

"Weren't you listening? The tallest mountain."

"Uh . . ."

"Everest," snorts Sonia Theraby. "Maybe he's asleep. Maybe he's eaten too much."

I glare at her.

"That will do, thank you, Sonia," says Ms. Price. "But, Drew, I do wish you would pay a little more attention."

I am paying a lot of attention to Ms. Price out of one eye. I am paying a lot of attention to Queeg with the other. It's giving me a headache.

Ms. Price draws a huge circle on the blackboard and marks the top of it "N."

"Now, this is a compass," says Ms. Price. "We need it to find Mount Everest. If the top of the compass is north, what is the other end?"

I see Queeg sitting up with sudden interest. I quickly throw him a "stop" sign.

"Drew?" says Ms. Price.

"Uh." I am trying to remember what the question was. "Uh, the bottom," I say.

Ms. Price closes her eyes. A bunch of Sonia's friends make noises like a tree full of monkeys. Then the principal calls Ms. Price, so she puts a lot of letters on the compass, tells us to copy them and leaves us alone.

"Duh, it's got to be the bottom," says Sonia, in her dumb voice. "'Because it isn't the top."

I show Sonia my fist, and I realize that I am making a dangerous sign again. I look around for Queeg, waving the "stop" sign.

"Watch out, he's going berserk again!" squeals Sonia.

I find Queeg. He's decided to improve Ms. Price's work on the blackboard again. I rush up, shouting, "No, Queeg!"

I am pulling at the little monster at the top of the blackboard, but he's pulling me around and around. He's as fast as Sir Harry with a stolen fish. Finally I swat him from the blackboard. He bounces on Ms. Price's table. I grab him by a leg. Then I look up, and the entire class is staring at me.

"Wild," Joe says with a funny look on his face.

I wiggle the fingers of my free hand at everyone and put Queeg behind my back. Yes, I know that nobody can see Queeg but me. I keep on forgetting. Anyway, they are not looking at me. They are staring at the blackboard. I turn around.

There is no compass any more. I mean, the big circle is still there on the blackboard, but you have to look for it. The big circle is now the fat belly of a huge monster with flapping ears and a curling tail, and it's staring at me. I leap for the eraser, but I can hear someone coming, clip-clip-clip, down the hall.

I wipe at an ear on the blackboard, but my nerves are all shot. I run to my desk just as Ms. Price reaches the door. I shove Queeg down in front of me, waving my finger before his great ugly nose.

"Why do you do this to me?" I hiss at Queeg.

Ms. Price stops at the door and squeals as though a group of mice were running over her feet. She points at the monster on the blackboard, and her finger wobbles all over the place as she says something like "Sha—soo—wha—tsah!"

Queeg purrs in my hands.

Ms. Price finally catches up with her tongue. "Who did *this* thing to my compass? This disgusting piece of mindless vandalism!"

I stare at Queeg. Queeg blinks happily at me. Joe looks at his fingers, and some of the girls look out the window. Even Shay snorts at the pencil in his hand. Everyone is trying to protect me. Except Sonia.

Sonia is grinning at me. Ms. Price looks at Sonia. "Drew? You did this? *You?*"

Okay, what can you do, eh? Say, "Oh no, Ms. Price, I was trying to *save* your great compass. All the damage was done by this horrible little monster in my hands. Yes, yes, I know you can't see him. Nobody can see him, except me. . . ." Hah! You're doomed, no matter what you say.

So you mumble.

"What did you say, Drew?"

"Sort of . . ."

"Have you lost your mind, Drew? Well, you can come up here, *now*, and clean up your mess."

I stand up. "You're a stinking little animal, you know that?" I hiss at Queeg. Queeg smirks back.

"Words will never hurt me . . ." Sonia says softly. Sonia has ears like radar.

"And you'll get yours too," I mutter.

"And, Drew Peters . . ." Ms. Price raises her voice. "You will stay after school and write fifty times on the blackboard, 'I must not write on the blackboard.'"

"Fifty times?" I say faintly.

"Fifty times. That will teach you to draw on my lesson."

I step past Sonia's desk and she lifts her nose and wrinkles it. I would love to pull it, but not here, not now. Suddenly she blinks and jerks her head back. I frown at her, then Joe crosses his eyes and turns away. Shay coughs, goes red and says, "Wow!"

Ms. Price frowns. "Is there something wrong, class?" Then: "Oh dear," and steps back, flicking her handkerchief at the air.

I look back at Queeg and he is looking absolutely innocent, so I know he has done something. Then I sniff.

"Oh," I say.

Imagine a barrelful of fish left in the sun for a week. And add two dozen eggs that were rotten a month ago, a stable for a hundred horses that has not been cleaned for a year . . .

Well, you get the idea. Sniff in Ms. Price's class and that is what you sniff. Kids are dredging up

old lunchbags and breathing into them for relief, kids are sliding away from me like I am a bomb, kids clutch their throats and fall into the aisle.

"This is terrible," pants Ms. Price. "Open the windows!"

The windows are flung open and Joe—my heroic friend—accidentally falls into the flowerbed outside.

"No, not enough," Ms. Price whispers weakly.

"Abandon shi—ah—evacuate the classroom. Orderly, orderly, don't crush. . . . Easy does it!"

The classroom is emptied in about thirty seconds. Queeg buzzes into the open air and settles on a branch above Ms. Price's head.

Ms. Price buries her nose in a flower for a minute, until she sees me. "You couldn't have—no, no you—that's ridiculous. Isn't it?" And she looks at me with wide eyes.

12

The King Kong Bit

Finally I get out of school and walk home. Dad is sitting in the sun, painting his plane.

"Hello, Drew, what do you think?" He holds the plane up to the light. He's almost purring.

"Hey, great!"

And it is, too. The propeller now sits on the bullet nose of a gleaming red-and-gold racing machine. It is only sitting in Dad's hand, but it looks like an eagle about to pounce.

"Well, it's ready to fly." Dad blows on the paint he has just finished putting on.

"Now? Really now?" I am moving around so much that Queeg falls off my shoulder.

"Why not? Come on." Dad pulls himself up from his chair and marches us off to the vacant lot.

I see that Queeg is creeping past Mrs. Brown's place, so I just have to bark a couple of times. Of course that brings the giant mutt to the gate. I almost have to run, but it's worth it to watch Queeg roll himself into a ball and bounce away down the street.

We stop in the middle of the vacant lot and Dad places his plane on the ground.

The vacant lot used to be a factory, but the owners tore it down and left only a half-wrecked chimney. Then they went away to figure out what to do next. So people use the lot to fly kites, kick balls around, play with dogs, or test-fly wild model planes.

Dad starts to sweep the ground in front of the plane with his hand, and I help him before I get yelled at.

"Qherrilif?" says Queeg, but I ignore him.

"Now, we'll see." Dad picks up the plane and fiddles with it before spinning the propeller with his finger. The tiny engine roars into life, and for

a moment the plane looks like it will haul Dad into the sky. Queeg tumbles away and stares at the plane.

Dad pulls the remote control panel from his pocket, adjusts things and places the plane on the ground. Then he jumps back and the plane is snarling, bouncing away from him.

Straight at Queeg.

"Eep!" he says and scrambles out of the way. He bounces into the air and flies. The plane bounces into the air and flies. Queeg flaps his wings so fast they drone. The plane roars and zooms towards the clouds. The propeller singes Queeg's tail, and he yells as he claws sideways. The plane sweeps high over the vacant lot and Queeg hides on the top of the chimney.

I laugh.

Dad looks sideways. "What's so funny?"

"Nothing, Dad. Just thought of something . . ."

"Oh." Dad works on the control panel and the plane loops the loop, flies just above the ground and flies above us upside down.

I am making "brummbroom" sounds and I move my hands as if I am *in* the plane, flying it.

"Hey, Drew." Dad is grinning at me. "You want to take over?"

"Who, me? I don't know how to . . ."

"Ah, it's easy. Come on."

I hold the control panel with Dad standing over me, and it's easier than riding a bike! I'm up there with the plane and *I'm* looping the loop, banking, diving, climbing. Dad steps back and I am flying solo.

Then I see Queeg on the top of the chimney.

Like King Kong. You know the movie: this huge gorilla climbs a skyscraper and has a fight with some planes. The planes win.

I am looking at Queeg and remembering all the trouble he's gotten me into. The bite on Sonia's leg, the stink in the class, the blackboard drawing, the game on the computer . . . I fly at him, making machine-gun sounds.

Queeg topples into the chimney as I zoom past.

He pulls himself back, and I dive at him with the engine shrieking. He scrambles across the top of the chimney, falls again—this time on the outside. He saves himself with a single claw. I pull out of my dive and soar into the sky.

He wobbles to his webbed feet and looks up at my fighter plane. I turn for another attack.

And then the horrible little monster jumps at me! He buzzes his butterfly wings and catches the plane and rides it like a pony. The engine shrieks, but it is only a very small engine, not meant to pull

64

a basketball-sized lump of ice cream and bananas.

The plane dips and shakes in the air. It begins to dive, and the engine screams.

"Get off, Queeg! Get off!"

"Yermonin!" Queeg squeals.

"What are you doing?!" Dad yells in my ear.

The plane is now aimed straight at the ground, its propeller dragging it down faster and faster. Queeg is climbing onto its tail.

"Give it to me!" Dad snatches the control panel and wrestles with it.

Queeg flaps from the plane, but it is too late.

The shining red-and-gold racing plane shatters on the stony ground.

Dad grabs my shoulder, almost crushing it for a moment. "You . . . you . . ." He is breathing through his teeth and his face is going purple.

"Sorry, Dad," I say, but that isn't going to get me anywhere. I am going to have to live on bread and water for ten years—if I live long enough to eat.

"Gark . . .!" Dad says deep in his throat, a horrible choking sound. Then he looks at the control panel in his hand and lets go of me.

I realize I am saved only because *he* had the control panel when the plane finally crashed, and he couldn't fly the plane either.

Dad walks over to the wreck. He kneels, picking

through the fragments. The propeller, the engine, the sweeping wings, the crimson tail—they are all gone, all part of a spread of splinters and bits of metal.

Then I look up and Queeg is watching, grinning in triumph.

I realize then that I must get rid of Queeg before he gets rid of me. . . .

13

The Escape Plot

All right, how do you get rid of an invisible, smelly creature that can fly? Next day, with Dad still trying to figure out what happened, I sit on the curb and try to figure it out.

Queeg sees a lizard scuttling after an ant. The lizard eyes the ant, flicks its blue tongue, and the ant is gone. Queeg eyes the lizard, licks the air, and the lizard is gone.

"The trouble with you, Queeg," I say, shaking my finger, "is that you are a little monster. A real little monster. Not a nice little monster, not a cute little monster, but just a stinking little monster."

Queeg belches and rubs his belly happily.

"You've got to go."

Joe rides up on his brand-new silver bicycle. "Who are you talking to?"

"Nothing, no one. That's a great bike. Hey . . ." I get to my feet and stroke the handlebars. "Can I have a ride on it?"

"Well . . ."

"Look, I'll be so careful. Ten gears, wow, what

does it feel like?"

"Oh, all right . . ." Joe swings down from the bike and shoves his helmet on my head. "But watch it."

"Sure, sure." I leap on the bike. "Be back soon." Then I grin sideways at Queeg. "Goodbye!"

Queeg blinks at me, puzzled, and then I am off. The wheels hum on the road. My feet on the pedals take great leaps. The wind washes through my hair—I am flying again! Queeg is trying to keep up, but he is a fat bumblebee and I am a soaring eagle. Queeg begins to catch me on a long slope, but I work the ten gears to keep most of the speed up. Then I am on the top of a steep hill. Queeg is about ten yards away from me for a moment, then I push down hard.

The tires are burning the asphalt. In seventh gear, my feet are slowing down while the road blurs past. In eighth gear, the wind batters my ears. In tenth gear, I am passing a motorcycle. Around a corner, through a clump of trees and toward a bridge. I get a dangerous wobble. For a moment I can see a stream before me, not the bridge, and I jam on the brakes. I skid across the road and the tires are smoking. I bang my knee on the concrete side of the bridge. I get over the bridge still speeding. Queeg is out of sight.

I stop, and Queeg is not there. The birds are chirping. The sun is shining. The sky is blue. The flowers are blooming. Queeg is not there. Great!

I ride slowly back to Joe, feeling that a huge load has been taken off my back. It was so easy to shake off Queeg. I should have done it earlier.

Joe is leaning against a lamppost, looking the other way, so I ring the bell.

"Where've you been?" he says, and then, suspiciously: "I can smell burning rubber."

"It is a great bike. You wouldn't believe how fast it can go. . . ."

Then I hear a heavy buzz in the air. I look up and there's Queeg wobbling down from the top of the lamppost.

14
Caught Again, and Again

Oh, I try again. Many times.

Ms. Price takes us to the zoo. She spends a lot of the time staring at me and warning that if anyone does anything to disturb the zoo he will be led home by the ear. I glare at Queeg and Queeg wurfles quietly to himself.

Anyway we go into the aviary, a huge birdcage full of trees, vines, flowers, ferns—and, of course, thousands of flashy birds. Just the spot for a small monster. We go in through a revolving door. I make sure that Queeg and I are the last to go out. Or at least that *I* am the last to go out.

Queeg is showing interest in a peacock. I pick up a rock before I step into the revolving door. I turn the door until I am out, then quick as a flash I jam the rock against the door, trapping Queeg in the cage with the thousands of birds. I run to catch up with the class.

"What have *you* been up to?" Sonia says.

"Nothing, nothing at all," I say, and wiggle my eyebrows.

Another five seconds and we are out of sight of the aviary. Another ten minutes and we will have left the zoo and its horrible secret. I will never come back again.

Except that the peacock shrieks as if somebody is chasing it with an ax. Ms. Price makes sure I am nowhere near the peacock and runs back into the aviary. She kicks the rock aside without seeing it. The peacock quiets down. She comes out with a frown and a peacock feather, followed by Queeg.

As we walk past a cage, Queeg snatches a banana from a smug monkey and throws it to me. I catch it without knowing what I am doing. Sonia squeals, "You didn't!" A tribe of monkeys throw peanut shells at me. . . .

So it goes on. Mom and Dad take me on a trip to the country, with Queeg. We stop to look at a bunch of cows. Queeg starts to swing on the tail of one. So I leap back into the car and lock the doors, letting in only Mom and Dad. They think I've gone crazy, but we drive off. With Queeg sitting on the hood . . .

I go to the beach and catch waves on my boogie board. With Queeg beside me, riding his big webbed feet . . .

We go to the movies, me carrying a big box. I give Queeg a bag of popcorn, and while he is snorting away, I duck out with my box. It contains an old hat, Dad's trench coat, a beard, and dark glasses—all of which I put on. I then walk quietly to the side exit.

Outside are Sonia and her friends. They see me.

I have never heard girls laugh so loudly and for so long. I walk home, tripping in the long coat, the hat tilting over my eyes.

And in the air above me there is the sound of mosquitoes. . . .

15

The Last Try

My last desperate attempt to get rid of Queeg starts in Ms. Price's class. I am looking at Queeg, waiting for his next bright idea. The kids are sitting as far away from me as they can. Ms. Price is watching me like I am a tiger. Everything is normal.

"Are you paying attention, Drew?" Ms. Price says.

"Oh yes." Queeg is very quiet. Even his eyes are closed.

"Then tell me what you can expect to find in Alaska?"

He might even be asleep! "Uh, palm trees . . ."

Sonia laughs.

"*Palm* trees? And you'd expect to find sandy beaches at the North Pole? Yes, Sonia?"

Sonia is waving her arm as if the school's on fire. "Huge glaciers, blizzards, mountains, polar bears . . ."

"Yes, yes, Sonia."

I lean toward Joe. "Where is Alaska anyway?"

He shrugs. "Somewhere near the North Pole. Why, you want to go there?"

And then it comes to me. "Nah. I want to send someone there."

I stay after school with Sonia, who is fiddling with some project or other. I find an empty box which used to be full of books and put it next to Queeg.

"Who said you could use that?" Sonia says.

"Ms. Price said." And she did too. Sort of. I asked if I could use any of the old boxes lying around for a project on Alaska, and she frowned but she said yes.

I pick up Queeg very gently and put him in the box.

Sonia looks at me oddly and comes over and looks into the box. Queeg is sleeping peacefully.

"It's empty," she says. "Stop making that sound, Drew."

I quickly close the box and tape it shut very tightly.

"Making an empty box? What are you doing?"

"It's a package." I grab a thick black pen and write ALASKA on the side of the box.

"Oh, it's a *pretend* package."

I look at her, very low, with beady eyes. "Yes."

"But where are you going to send it to? Alaska

is a big place."

"Oh, somewhere very little." I look in an atlas and write VALDEZ above ALASKA. Then I write 53 MAIN STREET above Valdez. I figure that every place has a Main Street. It's got to have fifty-three houses. Otherwise the street would not be *main*. Who needs smart-aleck girls like Sonia?

"Who are you going to send your empty box to, then?" Sonia practically yells into Queeg's ear.

Oh. You have to send the parcel to a *person* living at 53 Main Street, Valdez, Alaska.

"Uh . . . um. George Washington."

So George Washington of 53 Main Street, Valdez, Alaska, is going to get a box in the mail. Sorry, Mr. Washington, but it's your turn. . . .

Except it doesn't turn out that way.

16

A New Home

Sonia peers over my shoulder. "It's still a dumb project. Are you going to give this box to Ms. Price? Big deal."

She snatches the box from my desk and staggers back. "Hey, this is heavy!" Then she drops it.

There is a yelp from the box. I know I have failed. I will be followed by a smart little monster forever. I rise from the desk and run for the door.

"Hey!" Sonia yells after me. "You can't leave that here."

I turn. Queeg shoves his feet through the bottom of the box, as I knew he would, and plods toward me.

"How do you do that?" Sonia shrieks in amazement.

Of course. To her it looks like the box has lifted from the floor and is now walking to me. "It's a trick," I say, without thinking much about it.

"Oh come on . . ."

And suddenly I have an idea. "Oh, anyone can

do it."

"Must be easy if *you* can do it."

"It is. You can have it, but I must warn you, you may not want to keep it. You cannot tell anyone about it. It will cost you five cents. . . ."

These days I sometimes see floating chairs and hear distant giggles, but they have nothing to do with me. They are Sonia's. She has become the naughtiest girl in school, especially since she somehow connected the school speaker system to a rock station. Nobody knew how to turn it off. Then there was the time she was suspected of hanging the other girls' backpacks from a tall tree.

She often stares angrily at me from her desk. I just ignore her. It's her problem.

Except things are a bit dull around here now.

Sometimes, just sometimes, I wish Queeg was back with me. . . .